What Should Riley Do?

randomhousekids.com

ISBN 978-0-7364-3429-4 (trade) — ISBN 978-0-7364-8242-4 (lib. bdg.)

Printed in the United States of America

10 9 8 7 6 5 4 3 2 1

What Should
Riley Do?

By Tracey West

Illustrated by the Disney Storybook Art Team

Random House 🏠 New York

Welcome to Headquarters!

Meet the Five Emotions who live inside Riley's mind: Joy, Sadness, Anger, Disgust, and Fear. They help Riley make decisions. What should Riley wear today? What should she eat? Where should she sit during lunch? Riley's Emotions are with her every step of the way.

Now you can get inside Riley's mind, too! In this book, you'll see what life was like for Riley in Minnesota, before she moved to San Francisco. You'll meet her best friend, Meg, and watch them play on an ice hockey team.

As Riley moves through life, you can help the Emotions guide her decisions throughout her day. See if you can keep Riley's Islands of Personality running smoothly, and keep track of how many happy memories you can make for her. There are lots of happy memories to be made!

Beep! Beep! Beep!

The alarm clock in Riley Anderson's bedroom flashes 6:45 a.m. Riley stirs in her sleep.

Inside Riley's mind, Joy wakes up the other Emotions.

"Rise and shine!" Joy calls out. "It's a brand-new day, and it's going to be a great one!"

Joy's big blue eyes are gleaming with excitement. Her whole body glows with happy energy.

Anger is a short red Emotion. He stomps into Headquarters. He's wearing a suit and tie, and the top of his head is flat.

"Why does Riley have to wake up so early?" Anger complains. "It's still dark out!"

"Isn't that nice, though?" Joy responds. "Riley can see the stars when she wakes up."

A plump blue Emotion in glasses comes in next. "Poor Riley has to leave her soft, comfortable bed," says Sadness.

"But she gets to put on her super-soft,

comfortable sneakers!" says Joy excitedly.

A skinny purple Emotion with bulging eyes follows Sadness. "Do you think there's going to be a pop vocabulary quiz today?" Fear asks.

"If there is, Riley will do great!" says Joy. "'Great: adjective, of an extent, amount, or intensity considerably above the normal or average.' See? She studied so hard last night!"

Finally, a short green Emotion with perfect hair and long eyelashes walks in. "Um, Riley's breath is super gross," says Disgust. "She needs to brush her teeth, like, now."

"Riley never forgets to brush her teeth," Joy reminds her. "It's a minty burst of fresh-ness every day!"

"It is *way* too early for freshness," Anger snaps.

"It's never too early for freshness," says Joy. "Come on, I can tell it's going to be a great day. It's the first day of spring!"

"And this is Minnesota," says Disgust. "Which means it's still freezing out."

"Well, the cold air keeps Riley's mind sharp," says Joy. "She's the smartest ten-year-old in all of Eden Prairie. And don't forget, Riley and Meg both made the ice hockey spring travel team. Practice starts soon."

Fear shudders. "Slippery ice. Fast-moving pucks. Players swinging sticks. I don't know why Riley loves to throw herself in the face of icy danger."

"She does it because it's fun," Joy says.

Joy looks up at the large screen in front of her. On it, the Emotions can see everything Riley sees.

"Oatmeal for breakfast. Yum!" Joy says.

Disgust frowns. "Plain oatmeal is so boring. Couldn't Mom get the apple-cinnamon kind once in a while?"

"Apple-cinnamon or not, oatmeal gives

Riley the energy she needs to tackle the day," Joy says.

Then Joy looks out the window in the back of Headquarters. The window looks out over the Mind World—the rest of Riley's mind. Joy smiles when she sees that all of Riley's Islands of Personality are happily aglow: Goofball Island, Friendship Island, Family Island, Hockey Island, and Honesty Island. These islands make Riley the special girl she is!

Past the islands, Joy can almost see the shelves of Long Term Memory, which store the memories Riley makes every day. Most of them are golden yellow—which means they're happy memories. And that makes Joy happy.

Riley eats her breakfast, brushes her teeth, puts on her coat, and goes outside just before the school bus pulls up.

The Emotions spend a busy day helping Riley make decisions.

In social studies class, Mr. Cooper asks if anyone knows three rights guaranteed by the Declaration of Independence.

"Riley knows this!" Joy cries.

"Are you sure?" asks Fear nervously.

"Who even cares?" asks Disgust. "That was, like, a thousand years ago."

"Riley cares. She's got this!" says Joy.

Riley raises her hand.

"Life, liberty, and the pursuit of happiness," says Riley, and Mr. Cooper nods.

"Good job, Riley!" he says.

"Awesome!" cries Joy, high-fiving Fear.

At lunchtime, Riley is sitting with her best friend, Meg, when Eric Fischer comes up to the table.

"Hey, Riley, I'll trade you this bag of salt and vinegar chips for your cookies," he says.

Disgust makes a face. "Salt and vinegar? That sounds like something you clean drains with, not eat."

Riley politely refuses, and Disgust breathes a sigh of relief.

By the end of the day, the choices get a little more confusing. Riley's English teacher stops her in the hallway.

"Riley," says Ms. McGuire, "are you trying

out for the school play this afternoon?"

"School play? That sounds like fun!" Joy says, running up to the screen.

"Um, I didn't know about it," Riley says.

"Well, I'd like you to think about it," says Ms. McGuire. "I think you'd be great onstage."

"Of course Riley would be great onstage!" says Joy.

Ms. McGuire walks away, and Sara comes up to Riley. She's Riley's friend, and she can be a bit shy.

"Riley, I hope you try out," Sara whispers. "I'm scared to do it, but if you sign up, too, I won't be so scared."

Before Riley can answer, Meg walks up.

"Hey, are you coming to my house after school?" she asks.

"I don't know," Riley says. "Ms. McGuire asked me to—"

Just then, Riley's phone makes a honking

noise. She has gotten a text from her dad.

GOT OFF WORK EARLY. WANT TO GO SKATING?

"Ice-skating! That's even more fun than being in a play," says Joy.

"But we'll let Sara down, and that will be sad," Sadness points out.

"I think being in a play is a bad idea," says Fear. "What if Riley gets the part and then forgets her lines onstage?"

"Meg is Riley's best friend," says Disgust. "Ditching friends is not cool."

"But Meg should understand that Riley has something *else* to do," fumes Anger. "Isn't that how friends are supposed to act?"

Which Emotion should Riley follow?

If Riley tries out for the play, go to page 79.

If Riley hangs out with Meg, go to page 43.

If Riley goes along with her dad, go to page 21.

Riley tries to plow through the two defenders in front of her. But the defenders won't let her past. One of them swipes the puck from her. Before Riley can stop her, she speeds away.

Smoke comes out of Anger's ears. "Nooooo!"

The defender brings the puck down the ice and passes it to one of the Penguin wings. She shoots. Riley watches, helpless, as the puck slams into the goal.

Seconds later, the buzzer goes off. The Penguins win!

"This is so depressing," sobs Sadness.

"Ew, stop crying on me," says Disgust.

Riley skates off the ice, and Coach Cricket nods at her. "Nice effort, Riley. Thanks for listening and passing to Libby."

Riley grins.

"All right! Coach Cricket likes us!" says Joy.

THE END

"Um, would it be okay if you just trimmed it a little?" Riley asks.

Sienna shrugs. "Whatever you want."

Riley looks at Mom.

"That's fine, Riley," Mom says.

Sienna trims Riley's hair. Riley walks out of the salon with a smile on her face.

"I'm glad you were honest with me back there," Mom says.

"Well, as long as we're being honest, do you think we could go to the rock-climbing place while we're here?" Riley asks. "I mean, it's fun to get a haircut and new clothes, but we haven't been rock climbing in a while."

Mom grins. "Sure thing," she says.

Joy grins, too. "Being honest really pays off!"

"Oh, does it?" Fear asks. "We're about to be hanging fifty feet off the ground on a fake plaster wall.

You know what the payoff to that is?" He shudders before continuing. "A broken leg!"

"Not to mention that she'll get all sweaty," says Disgust.

Joy shakes her head. "Sometimes you guys are just no fun."

THE END

Meg comes back into the room.

"So a text popped up on your phone from Emily," Riley says. "Something about a party?"

"Oh yeah, she's having a party," Meg says. "Why, weren't you invited?"

"No," Riley replies. "Why didn't you tell me about it?"

Meg shrugs. "I didn't think it was a big deal. Sorry."

"So . . . are you going?" Riley asks.

"Yeah, why not?" Meg replies.

"WHY NOT?" fumes Anger. "Because Emily didn't invite us, *that's* why not!"

"Meg doesn't care about our feelings at all," whimpers Sadness.

"You guys. This is the moment. This is the moment we realize we have no real friends," says Fear.

"Well, she didn't invite me," Riley says. "So I thought maybe you wouldn't go, either."

Meg looks uncomfortable. "I guess, but I mean, she invited me, and I like her, so . . ."

"Oh no, she did *not* just say that," says Disgust.

Anger's head bursts into flames. "HOW CAN MEG LIKE SOMEBODY WHO DOESN'T LIKE US?"

"It's just, if it were *me*, and Emily didn't invite *you*, I wouldn't go," says Riley.

"You wouldn't?" asks Meg, like she doesn't believe her.

"No, I wouldn't. Because I'm a *real* friend," Riley says.

Meg looks hurt.

"Quick! We hurt Meg's feelings! We have to apologize!" says Joy.

"No way!" says Anger. "It's the truth!"

If Riley apologizes to Meg, go to page 87.

If Riley doesn't apologize, go to page 107.

Riley types on her cell phone.

LET'S GO SKATING. ARE YOU PICKING ME UP?

YES! DON'T GET ON THE BUS, Dad texts back.

"Hooray! Skating!" Joy cries.

Fear shudders. "I hope the ice isn't too slippery today."

"Ice is always slippery. It's ice," Anger points out.

Riley turns to Meg. "Hey, Meg, my dad got off work early and wants to go skating. Do you want to come, too?"

"That's okay, I'm not in the mood," Meg says. She smiles. "Say hi to your dad for me."

In Headquarters, Anger looks triumphant. "I *told* you she would understand."

The final bell rings. Riley runs through the hallways and out of the school. She's so excited. She spots her dad's car in the parking lot and races toward him.

"Dad!" she cries, opening the door.

"Hey, Riley," Dad says. "Your skates are in the back. We're going straight to the rink."

Riley grins. "Thanks! You're the best!"

It's not quite cold enough to go to their favorite lake, so Dad drives to the Ice Palace, an indoor rink near the mall. It's nice and frosty inside—just the way Riley likes it. She quickly puts on her skates. Soon she and her dad are out on the ice.

Dad skates a perfect circle and then ends with a twirl, putting both arms above his head like a professional figure skater.

Riley giggles. "Show-off!"

"Come on, Riley, give it a try!" Dad urges.

Riley skates in a circle. She loves how fast she can move on the ice. Then she tries to spin into a twirl, too. She raises her arms in the air and wiggles her fingers.

"Woo-hoo!" Riley cheers.

"Why is she cheering? We nearly fell and

broke our neck!" says Fear. "It was awful!"

"But we had so much fun doing it!" Joy says.

Riley and Dad skate until it's almost dinnertime. On the ride home, Dad says, "Hey, Riley, I'm going to the computer expo on Saturday. Want to come?"

Inside Headquarters, Disgust says, "Ugh, no thanks. Welcome to Boresville, USA."

"But it's Dad," says Joy. "He can make anything fun."

"Sure," says Riley.

When they get home, Mom is setting the table.

"Did you two have a good time?" she asks.

"Yes!" Riley and Dad say together.

"Riley, I know I've been working a lot lately," says Mom. "I'd like to make it up to you. How about we go to the mall on Saturday?"

"Are you kidding me? We have to choose between Mom and Dad?" says Fear.

Sadness sighs. "Either way, we're going to let someone down."

"Oh, come on, you guys. They won't be disappointed," says Joy. "We just have to figure out which sounds like more fun!"

If Riley spends Saturday with Dad, go to page 31.

If she spends the day with Mom, go to page 74.

"Um, it's great, Mom," says Riley. "A pink wolf. Sure, why not?"

The next two weeks are really busy as everyone gets ready for the play. On opening night, Riley slips on her wolf costume. Riley's mom has cut the bunny ears short so that they look like wolf ears. She's replaced the bunny tail with a long, furry pink wolf tail. There's black makeup on Riley's nose.

"You look so cute!" says Sara.

"I'm not supposed to look cute. I'm supposed to look scary!"

Everybody at school comes to see the play. When Riley walks onstage, everyone laughs.

"So much for having a social life," Disgust says with a groan.

"Keep laughing and we'll climb off this stage and give you a taste of pink fuzzy fury!" Anger yells.

Riley growls and roars and huffs and puffs

and blows the audience away. She does a great job. But at school on Monday, Alex Whitman points at her in the hallway.

"Hey, Pinky!" he says.

Riley stops. "Who, me?"

"Yeah, you, Pinky!" says Michael Garcia.

Riley blushes.

"Who are you calling Pinky?" Anger fumes.

Disgust glares at Joy.

"Yeah, um, maybe next time we'll be honest with Mom," Joy says.

THE END

Sven Carlsson is staring at Riley. "Come on, eat up! Rebound Broccoli Bites are my favorite snack of all time!"

"We have to try them!" cries Joy.

"Nooooooooo!" wails Disgust. She reaches for the controls, but Anger and Fear hold her back.

Riley picks up a piece of broccoli and puts it in her mouth. She chews, then swallows it.

"They're great, right?" Sven asks.

"Hold back the barf!" Fear yells, and Riley forces herself to smile.

"Delicious," Riley lies.

Sven turns to Mom and Dad. "Mind if I get a selfie with this little hockey star of yours?"

"Okay with you, Riley?" Dad asks.

"Of course!" says Riley. She wiggles out of the booth and poses with Sven while he takes a picture.

Sven posts the photo online. At school on

Monday, everybody is talking about it. At lunch, a bunch of kids surround Riley's table.

"Do you know Sven personally?"

"What's he like?"

Riley answers everyone's questions. Nobody is talking about Emily's party.

"Riley's a celebrity," says Disgust happily. "I guess it was worth it eating that broccoli. But never again!"

Another happy memory rolls into the vacuum tube. . . .

THE END

Riley sees Coach Cricket out of the corner of her eye. She passes the puck to Libby. Libby shoots it into the Penguins' goal—and scores!

"Great assist, Riley!" Joy cheers.

The Penguins fight back hard. They pass the puck back and forth across the ice. Then one of the Penguins shoots—and the game is tied!

"Come on! We've got to win this one!" Anger yells.

Now Meg has the puck and she passes it to Libby. Libby passes it to Riley. Riley starts to go for the goal. Suddenly, the Penguins' defense is all over her.

Riley has to think fast. In front of her, two Penguins are blocking her path to the goal. She might be able to bank left—but another player is quickly skating in that direction.

"Plow through those two in front of us, Riley!" Anger yells.

"Go around them!" says Fear.

"Decisions are so stressful," Sadness cries.

"Ugh. Is this game ever going to be over?" whines Disgust.

If Riley plows forward, go to page 16.

If Riley goes around them, go to page 56.

"Mom, Dad already asked me to go to the computer expo with him," Riley says. "Can we go to the mall some other time?"

"Of course, honey," Mom says.

Joy lets out a happy cheer. "Road trip!"

Fear shudders. "You mean we get to ride down a highway in a tiny metal box next to giant speeding eighteen-wheelers? Can't we just stay home?"

Saturday morning, Riley and Dad get up early and hit the road.

"You're going to love the computer expo, Riley," Dad says. "There are all kinds of games you can test."

"Any hockey games?" Riley asks.

"I'm not sure, but we'll find out," Dad replies.

"How long till we get there?" Riley asks.

Dad looks at the clock on the dashboard. "About forty-five minutes."

Forty-five minutes later, they're still not

there. Then an hour passes. They're still driving.

"What is going on?" Anger fumes, pacing. "Why aren't we there yet?"

"Dad, are you lost?" Riley asks.

"No . . . I mean, maybe . . . I mean, yes," Dad admits. "I must have taken the wrong exit."

They're not on the highway anymore—they're on a country road in the middle of nowhere. There's still snow on the ground, and it's white as far as Riley can see.

Then they notice a sign on the side of the road: COME TO THE FROG MUSEUM! YOU'LL HAVE A HOPPING GOOD TIME!

"Hey, what do you say we follow that sign?" Dad asks. "We're lost anyway."

"I want to have a hopping good time!" Joy says.

Disgust frowns. "Frogs? Ew, seriously?"

If Riley and Dad go to the Frog Museum, go to page 83.

If they go to the computer expo, go to page 104.

(continued from page 88)

Meg's mom drives Riley and Meg to Emily's party. As Meg rings the bell, Riley takes a package out of her coat pocket. Her mom helped her pick out earrings and a funny birthday card. She hopes Emily will like them.

Meg looks at the package. "What is that?"

"Emily's present," says Riley.

"But it's not her birthday," says Meg. "It's just a party. Like, a hang-out party."

"Oh," Riley says, a little confused.

"Quick! Destroy it!" Disgust cries, but she's too late. Emily opens the door.

"Come in," she says. "Is that for me?" she asks, noticing the present.

"I, um, thought it was your birthday," Riley says, handing it to her.

"Of course. Birthday parties are so ten-year-old," Emily says as she leads them inside.

"Did she just insult us?" Anger asks.

Sadness nods. "Should we lock ourselves in

the bathroom now and start crying?"

Emily leads Riley and Meg down some steps into the family room. The lights are turned down low, and loud pop music is playing. A bunch of girls from Riley's class are there, sitting around and talking.

"What kind of party is this? Where are the balloons?" asks Anger. "You can't have a party without balloons!"

"I bet there'll be some party games soon," says Joy.

But there are no games. Just girls sitting and talking. Which is okay, but Riley gets bored. She wanders over to the snack table and picks up a roll of aluminum foil. She tears off a sheet and starts folding it.

After a few minutes, Riley has fashioned a cool bracelet from the foil. Two girls walk over.

"Did you just make that?" asks Olivia.

"It's nice," says Beatrice.

"We had a foil fashion show in summer camp," says Riley. "You can make all kinds of stuff out of aluminum foil."

"Can I try?" Olivia asks.

Riley tears off a sheet for her. "See, you fold it like this."

A few minutes later, a small crowd has gathered around Riley. Emily notices.

"What's going on?" she asks.

"We're making foil accessories for a foil fashion show!" says Beatrice.

"What?" Emily sounds mad.

Riley hands her a necklace. "Here. I made this for you. It will match the earrings I got you."

Emily smiles. "Wow, that's really cool. Thanks."

Soon everybody is making foil fashions and modeling them down an imaginary runway in the family room.

"I'm glad you came, Riley," Emily says with a real smile.

"That's our Riley," says Joy. "If there's no fun around, she'll make it!"

A glowing happy memory rolls into the tube.

THE END

"That was a great first rehearsal," says Ms. McGuire. "See you all on Wednesday."

"I told you that being in the play would be fun," Joy tells the other Emotions.

"Maybe, but now Riley has to go straight to hockey practice," says Fear. "What if she doesn't get there in time?"

"She'll make it," Joy says confidently as Mom drives Riley to the rink.

When they arrive, Riley runs in and quickly changes into her hockey gear. She's the last one on the ice. Meg and the other members of her travel team—the Otters—are skating around, warming up.

Coach Cricket skates out onto the ice. Her long brown hair is pulled back into a ponytail.

"All right, girls!" she yells. "Pair up! Let's start with some drills."

The next hour and a half goes by quickly. Riley and her teammates practice passing to each other, controlling the puck, and stopping and starting on the ice.

Coach Cricket blows a whistle when the practice is over. "Looking good, team! See you on Wednesday."

"How are you holding up, Riley?" Mom asks when Riley gets back in the car.

"Great! We can take on anything!" says Joy.

Sadness sighs. "We are so tired we want to cry."

"And we're so sweaty. Ugh," adds Disgust.

"Don't tell Mom the bad stuff, or she'll make us quit the play!" says Fear.

Riley yawns. "I'm doing great, Mom."

That night, Riley falls asleep right after she finishes her homework. She's so tired! Tuesday she has a break, but

Wednesday she has play rehearsal and hockey practice again. Thursday is just hockey practice. Friday is both again.

At rehearsal on Friday, Riley is feeling pretty tired when she says her lines.

"Hey, little pigs, let me in. Or I'll, um . . ." Riley can't remember the line, so she makes something up. ". . . or you'll be sorry!"

Fear gasps. "Oh no, Riley forgot her line."

"How the heck is she supposed to remember all those lines anyway?" Anger fumes.

But everybody just laughs. It's no big deal.

At hockey practice later, Meg passes to Riley during a practice game. The puck whizzes right through Riley's legs. She misses it completely!

"Look alive, Riley!" Coach Cricket calls out.

"Oh, great. We must look like a dork," groans Disgust.

"Practice makes perfect," says Joy.

Finally, it's Saturday. Riley sleeps late.

"See, guys?" Joy asks. "Riley can relax this weekend. It all worked out."

"But she has a book report due Monday," Fear reminds her. "And she has her first game tomorrow."

"Riley can do it!" says Joy.

Then Riley gets a text from Meg. **WANT TO GO TO THE MOVIES TODAY?**

"Yes! We love going to the movies with Meg!" Joy cheers.

Fear starts to sweat. "But if we don't do our book report, we'll flunk out of school!"

Sadness sighs. "It's too bad Riley can't have fun with Meg."

"Why not?" fumes Anger. "Why can't we have some fun?"

If Riley goes to the movies with Meg, go to page 93.

If Riley stays home, go to page 115.

"Okay, I'll get the haircut," Riley says. Sienna spins the chair around so that Riley is facing a big mirror.

Fear covers his eyes. "I can't look," he says.

"I'm sure it won't be that bad," says Joy.

Sienna snips and snips Riley's hair. Riley closes her eyes. She's afraid to look. Finally, Riley opens her eyes.

"Oh. Maybe it *can* be that bad," says Joy.

Riley doesn't look like herself. Her hair is shorter on the left side and longer on the right.

Sadness starts to cry. "All that beautiful long hair—gone!"

"It's, um, stylish," says Mom, trying not to hurt Riley's feelings. Riley's eyes fill with tears.

Mom knows that Riley is upset. When they leave the salon, she takes her to pick out a new hat. Riley chooses a red beanie and pulls it down as far as it will go.

The next morning, Riley doesn't want to get out of bed.

"We can't go to school looking like this," says Disgust.

"But the hat is cute!" says Joy.

"Nobody wears hats to school," argues Disgust.

Riley knows she can't skip school, so she pulls on her hat and gets on the bus. A few blocks later, Meg gets on—and she's wearing a hat, too!

She sits down beside Riley. "Your mom told my mom about your haircut. I thought if we both wore hats, nobody would notice."

Riley doesn't feel so miserable anymore. "Thanks, Meg," she says, and then she giggles. "I'll show you my hair later. It's awful."

"Meg is the best friend ever!" says Joy.

THE END

Riley texts her dad to let him know she has plans with Meg. Then she turns to Sara.

"I don't think I want to try out for the play," she says. "But you should do it. I'm sure you'll be great."

Sara smiles shyly. "Thanks, Riley."

Riley and Meg take the bus to Meg's house. Meg's little brother, Eric, is watching TV in the living room. Meg's mom is in her office with the door open.

"Hi, girls!" she calls out. "I've got to finish this up before my deadline. I baked oatmeal cookies for you. They're in the kitchen."

"Thanks, Mom," says Meg.

Riley and Meg grab some cookies and go upstairs to Meg's room. They dump their backpacks on Meg's bed and sit on the floor.

"I still can't believe that Alex Whitman burped in Mr. Roman's class!" Meg says. She and Riley burst into giggles.

"I know! It was so loud!" Riley says.

"Serves him right," says Meg. "He's been calling me Freckle Face all year."

"Well, now you can call him Burp Face," Riley says, and they start giggling again.

Meg picks up her phone. "Did you see that video of the world's loudest burp?"

"Ew, gross!" says Disgust.

"Ew, gross!" says Riley.

Riley and Meg are laughing over the video when Eric comes to the door.

"Mom says you have to help me find my crayons," he says.

Meg sighs. "How do you keep losing them? Be right back, Riley."

Meg leaves, handing Riley her phone. Riley is watching the burping video again when a text pops up on the screen.

YAY! GLAD YOU CAN COME TO MY PARTY!

The text is from Emily Stevens.

"*Excuse* me? Emily Stevens? She didn't invite *us* to her party," says Disgust.

"Nobody loves us!" wails Sadness.

"Oh, come on, you guys, she probably just forgot," Joy says.

"But Meg never mentioned that she was invited to Emily's party," says Anger. "Why wouldn't she say anything?"

Riley hears Meg coming back up the stairs and puts down the phone.

"Riley should just ask Meg about it," says Joy. "She'll clear it right up."

"We can't do that! What if Meg gets mad that Riley read the text?" Fear asks.

If Riley asks Meg about the text from Emily, go to page 19.

If Riley keeps it to herself, go to page 95.

(continued from page 55)

Riley skates over to Meg. She raises her hands in the air and sings along to the song.

"Hey now!" Riley says.

Meg smiles. She raises her hands in the air.

"Hey now!" says Meg.

Riley and Meg start skating together, doing their goofy dance to the song. Soon they're cracking up.

"I'm really sorry," Riley says.

"Me too," says Meg.

"They made up!" Joy cheers.

"You mean we won't be alone and lonely forever?" Fear asks.

Joy smiles. "We'll always be friends with Meg."

THE END

"I have dress rehearsal that night," Riley says. Meg looks super sad. "But I'll go to your party. I wouldn't miss it."

Meg smiles. Riley feels good.

It's not easy breaking the news to Ms. McGuire.

"She's my best friend," Riley says. "Since we were, like, babies. I can't miss it."

Ms. McGuire nods. "Well, I expect you at all of our other practices, Riley. No more absences, okay?"

Riley nods. "Promise."

Riley works hard on the play over the next few days. She goes to Meg's party, which really is awesome. They go to the arcade and eat pizza. Then they go to the ice cream place for a giant sundae with candles in it.

The play is two days away. Riley puts on her wolf costume, which Mom has dyed brown. It looks pretty cool.

When she's onstage, though, she keeps bumping into the three little pigs. The audience laughs.

"What is happening? Why are these pigs in the wrong place?" Anger yells.

Then Riley remembers. They changed the scene during one of the dress rehearsals. Riley practiced the new moves a few times, but she's mixed-up now and doing the old ones.

"It's all because we went to Meg's party," says Sadness.

At the end of the play, Riley and the other cast members go onstage. When Riley comes out, Meg stands up and cheers and whistles. Riley smiles.

"See? It doesn't matter that Riley bumped into a few pigs onstage. Meg will always be her friend," Joy says.

THE END

"I'll get a haircut," Riley says. "It's been a while."

Riley and her mom step inside the salon. Music is blaring from the speakers. The teenage girl at the front desk has white-blond hair with a blue streak running through it.

"Hey!" she says with a big smile. "Are you here for a haircut?"

"Yeah, I guess I am," Riley says, a little nervously.

"Sienna can take you," says the girl. "But first, you can get your hair washed."

Riley is whisked to the back of the salon. Her hair gets washed, and soon she's sitting in a metal chair with a towel around her. A stylist with spiky black hair walks up.

"Hi, I'm Sienna," she says. "You're adorable. So, are you ready to get rid of all that hair for the spring?"

"I, um . . ." Riley isn't sure.

Disgust rolls her eyes. "Nobody in our grade has short hair. She can't do this!"

Sienna holds up a picture of a model with a short haircut. It's slanted on both sides of the model's head. "This would be super cute on you."

"Oh, Riley, that is cute," says Mom. "What do you think?"

Riley looks in the mirror. She tries to imagine the short haircut on her.

"No way!" says Disgust.

"What if Riley ends up looking ridiculous?" asks Fear.

"Mom thinks it will be cute," says Joy. "We should trust her."

"And we don't want to disappoint Mom," adds Sadness.

If Riley gets the short haircut, go to page 41.

If Riley just gets a trim, go to page 17.

Riley knows Coach Cricket will be mad, but she doesn't trust Libby. She wants to win the game!

Riley swings, about to take a shot at the goal. But one of the Penguins skates right in front of her and blocks the shot! The Penguins have the puck! They take it down the ice and score.

Buzz! The game ends. The Penguins win!

Riley skates off the ice.

Coach Cricket shakes her head. "Riley, we need to talk about your sportsmanship," she says.

"Riley should have passed to Libby," Sadness says. "Coach is probably really disappointed in us."

"Well, it's only the first game," Joy reminds her. "Riley has the whole season to show her she's a great player!"

THE END

"Um, no thank you," Riley says politely.

Sven frowns. "Well, I guess my broccoli is not for everybody. Good luck with your team!"

Then Sven walks to another table. Riley sees him talking to a boy in a hockey jersey. It's Alex Whitman, from her school!

Alex eats the broccoli. Then Sven and Alex take a picture together.

"Did you see that?" asks Joy. "We should have eaten the broccoli."

"Well, I'm still glad we didn't," says Disgust.

But the next day, Riley finds out that Sven posted the photo of him and Alex online. Now Alex is a school celebrity.

"Who knew that eating broccoli could improve your social status?" asks Disgust.

"Does that mean we'll eat it now?" asks Fear.

"Never!" Disgust promises.

THE END

Riley lets Meg leave without saying good-bye.

For the rest of the day, the Emotions are trying to figure out what to do.

"Should we text her? I think we should text her," says Joy.

"She probably just wants some time alone," says Sadness.

"Why do we even care?" adds Disgust.

"We should just cut our losses. It's pretty obvious she doesn't want to be our friend ever again," says Fear.

"I keep saying it—SHE should be the one apologizing to US!" shouts Anger.

"Well, we have to do something," says Joy.

That night, Mom and Dad take Riley to the indoor skating rink to celebrate the hockey win. When Riley skates onto the ice, she sees

Meg across the rink. She's with her family—and Emily!

"Emily? She came here with *Emily*?" Anger can't believe it.

Riley skates around, ignoring Meg and Emily. Then the music changes.

"It's Riley and Meg's favorite song," says Joy. "They always skate to this song."

"Do you think Meg even remembers?" asks Sadness.

"Of course she does!" says Joy. "They just skated to it a few weeks ago. They always do that goofy dance."

Riley just keeps skating. She passes Meg and Emily on the ice. Riley can see it in Meg's eyes. She knows it's their song.

"Come on! Let's dance with Meg!" Joy urges.

"Are you kidding me? She's here with Emily. Emily, of all people!" Anger fumes.

If Riley skates up to Meg, go to page 46.

If Riley doesn't skate up to Meg, go to page 100.

(continued from page 30)

Riley banks to the left, avoiding the two defenders. Another Penguin is zipping toward her, but Riley is faster. She zooms past her until she has a clear shot at the goal.

Wham! Riley sends the puck flying toward the goal. The Penguins' goalie has to lunge to the right to stop it—but she isn't quick enough.

Whoosh! The puck hits the net. Riley scores!

Seconds later, the buzzer rings. The Otters win!

"What a great start to the season!" says Joy.

As Riley high-fives Meg, a golden sphere rolls into the vacuum tube. One more happy memory!

THE END

Riley pulls the blue lever.

Ding! Ding! Ding!

A loud bell rings. A siren wails. Blue lights flash in the studio. Then confetti falls down on Riley and Mom!

"Take cover!" Fear yells, diving under the control panel.

"It's okay," says Joy. "We won! We won!"

Riley and Mom are jumping up and down. Skip Watley walks over.

"Congratulations, Riley and Jill, you win *Splash!*" he says. "You've won a trip for the whole family to the Ice Hockey Museum!"

Riley high-fives Mom.

"Woo-hoo!" cheers Joy. She sees a gold memory roll into Headquarters. "Another happy memory!"

THE END

(continued from page 78)

Riley sees Sara again in art class.

"Um, Sara, I don't think I can hang out with you tomorrow," Riley says.

Sara looks down at her sneakers.

Sadness sighs. "I knew she would be crushed."

"We can make this better," says Joy.

"Maybe we could get together Saturday instead?" Riley asks.

Sara gives her a big smile. "Sure!"

"Whew!" says Fear. "We saved that one."

"Up top!" Joy says, and she high-fives him.

Outside Headquarters, in Mind World, Friendship Island glows brightly.

THE END

Riley takes a deep breath. "I'm not going. Emily obviously doesn't want me there. But you should go. I swear I won't be mad."

"You swear?" Meg asks.

Riley nods. "Promise."

Meg smiles. Riley is glad everything is okay.

But the night of Emily's party, Riley is feeling a little left out and bored. She's reading a magazine in her room when Dad knocks on the door.

"Get your coat on, kiddo," he says. "We're going to Sven Carlsson's for dinner!"

Riley practically bounces off the bed. Sven Carlsson is a famous ex-hockey player who opened a restaurant called Sven Carlsson's Kitchen when he retired.

"Hooray! It's Riley's favorite place to eat," says Joy.

"Do you think we'll see him there tonight?"

Riley asks her parents as they drive to the restaurant.

"Well, we haven't seen him yet," says Mom. "So let's not get our hopes up."

Joy's blue eyes are twinkling with excitement. "My hopes are up! I can't help it!"

When they get to the restaurant, a waitress in a hockey jersey shows them to their table. Hockey photos, hockey sticks, and hockey jerseys decorate the walls. Big-screen TVs show hockey games from the past featuring Sven.

Riley doesn't even need to look at the menu. "I'm getting the Championship Burger with Potato Pucks on the side," she announces.

"Good choice," says Dad, putting down his menu. Then his eyes get wide. "Riley! It's Sven!"

Riley turns her head. A big man with white hair is shaking hands with customers. Riley's mouth drops open.

"It's really him!" she cries.

Sven turns around and walks toward Riley's table.

"Oh my gosh! He's coming over! What will we say?" Fear cries.

"You guys. This man is our idol," says Disgust. "Let's not blow it."

"I like your hockey jersey, little lady," Sven says in a booming voice. He reaches out his hand and Riley shakes it. "Do you play?"

"Um, yeah," Riley says. Suddenly, she feels shy.

"Say something! Anything!" Disgust pleads.

"She's the center on her travel team," Mom says proudly.

"Well, that's wonderful!" Sven says. He motions to a waiter and then grabs something off his tray. "Here you go. Have some Rebound Broccoli Bites on me! Go ahead, try one!"

Disgust turns pale. "Did he say broccoli?"

"He sure did," says Joy.

Disgust folds her arms defiantly. "No way! No broccoli! It's disgusting!"

"But it's Sven Carlsson!" Anger protests.

"We can't hurt his feelings," Sadness moans.

"But what if we barf all over him?" Fear shrieks.

If Riley eats the broccoli, go to page 27.

If Riley refuses the broccoli, go to page 52.

(continued from page 72)

Riley pulls the red lever.

Splash! A shower of chocolate pudding falls from the ceiling and douses them.

"Noooooooooo!" cries Disgust.

Riley's goggles are covered with pudding. She takes them off so she can see. Pudding is dripping down Mom's face.

"Oh no! Mom's going to be furious!" Fear is worried.

But Mom smiles. She wipes some pudding from her cheek and tastes it.

"Mmm, yum," she says. Then she and Riley crack up. Riley is laughing so hard, she almost falls over.

"But Riley and Mom lost. They should be sad," Sadness says, confused.

"But they're having fun," says Joy, as a golden sphere rolls down the tube. "See? Even losing can be a happy memory!"

THE END

(continued from page 82)

The next day, Riley explains to Ms. McGuire that play rehearsal will interfere with hockey practice.

"I understand," says Ms. McGuire. "Good luck with hockey, Riley."

Then Riley talks to Sara, and she understands, too. Riley is pumped as she gets to her first practice for the ice hockey travel team, the Otters, that afternoon. She was top scorer on her school team, and she wants to impress her new coach and her other teammates.

Riley is the first one at practice. She changes into her hockey gear and skates onto the ice to warm up.

One by one, the other members of her team skate out. Riley recognizes most of them from school.

There's Meg, her best friend, who's also a great scorer. Then there's Olivia, who played goalie on her school team. Grace and Libby glide out next—they're best friends and always skate together.

Some of the girls are from other schools, and Riley doesn't recognize them.

"Do you think they're better than Riley?" Fear wonders.

"Everyone on the team is awesome," Joy says. "Or they wouldn't have made the travel team."

Then Coach Cricket skates out onto the ice. She's tall and wears her long brown hair in a ponytail.

"All right, Otters!" she says. "Pair up with a partner. I want to start with some drills."

Riley and Meg team up.

"This is so exciting!" says Joy.

Coach Cricket has the girls pass the puck back and forth as they skate across the ice. Then she puts out some cones and the players practice stopping and starting.

For the next drill, groups of three—a goalie, an offensive player, and a defensive player—compete against one another.

Riley starts on offense. She swoops toward the goal, avoiding Grace, who's blocking her. Then she swings and shoots the puck right past Olivia—and into the goal.

"Woo-hoo!" cheers Joy.

"Nice work, Riley!" Coach Cricket says.

Practice is over too soon. Riley can hardly wait until the next one on Wednesday. When she gets there, Coach Cricket has some news for the Otters.

"I'm sorry to report that Olivia, our goalie, has sprained her ankle," she says. "So I'd like to see some players try out for the position today. Riley, Madison, and Ava."

Fear shudders. "All those pucks whizzing toward Riley? No way! That's too dangerous!"

"But goalies get to wear cool-looking gear," Disgust points out.

If Riley tries out for goalie, go to page 110.

If Riley doesn't try out, go to page 97.

(continued from page 122)

"Is it a fun show?" Mom asks.

"Really fun," Riley says, and Mom smiles.

"Yes, we'll do it!" Mom tells Mindy.

"Wonderful! Follow me," Mindy says.

Riley and her mom follow Mindy to the *Splash!* studios on the third floor of the mall. Fear starts to get shaky.

"This is really happening. We're going to be on TV!" he says.

"On our favorite show!" Joy cheers.

It all happens really fast. Riley and her mom get tiny microphones clipped to their shirts. Mom has to fill out some forms. Then they go to a stage, where they stand behind a pole with a big red buzzer on top. Next to them, a dad and his son are in front of another buzzer.

"Places, everyone!" Mindy yells. "All right, lights, camera, action!"

A guy in a blue T-shirt and jeans jogs out in front of them. "Hi, I'm Skip Watley. Welcome to *Splash!* Today our contestants are Riley and her mom, Jill, and Max and his dad, Steve!"

The audience claps. Riley's hands start to sweat a little.

"We can't do this!" Fear cries.

"Yes we can!" Joy assures him.

"In our first round, Riley and Max will answer trivia questions, with the help of their parents," Skip says. "Here's our first question: Which hockey team won the Stanley Cup in 2010?"

Riley's not afraid anymore. She knows the answer! Her hand presses the buzzer.

"The Chicago Blackhawks!" she answers.

"Correct!" says Skip.

Riley and Mom breeze through the trivia questions. Riley is impressed that Mom knows the names of all four Beatles.

"Congratulations, Riley and Jill!" says Skip. "You move on to our obstacle course!"

Mindy rushes up with two pairs of goggles, two blue vests, and two blue helmets. She helps Riley and Mom put them on. Then she leads them to the obstacle course.

"Okay, Riley and Jill, you know how this works," Skip says. "You have sixty seconds to get through the obstacle course. If you get there in time, you can pull one of the levers. One of them leads to a prize. The other one leads to pudding. Are you ready?"

"Ready!" Riley and Mom say together.

"I am *not* ready!" protests Fear.

"Go!" yells Skip.

Riley and Mom run through the obstacle course. They belly-crawl through a tunnel and climb up a rope wall. They walk on a balance beam and hop from rock to rock across a fake pond. The clock is ticking.

Then Riley sees them—two levers. One red and one blue. She looks at the clock. Five seconds left.

"Which one, Riley?" Mom asks.

"I hope we pick the right one," says Sadness. "It will be awful if Riley doesn't win!"

If Riley pulls the blue lever, go to page 57.

If she pulls the red one, go to page 63.

During the half, Riley talks to Coach Cricket.

"Can I go back to being center?" Riley asks. "I don't think I want to be goalie anymore."

Coach Cricket frowns. "Riley, don't let the first half get you down."

"It's not that," Riley says. "It's just . . . I'm better at being center."

Coach nods. "If that's what you want, Riley, fine. I don't want you at the goal if your heart's not in it."

Coach Cricket puts Riley back in at center. But something doesn't feel right.

Sadness points out the window. "Look at Hockey Island. Is that a storm cloud?"

The Emotions look. A dark cloud is forming over Hockey Island.

"It's just one little cloud," says Joy. "Don't worry. This is just a bump in the ice. Riley will get her hockey groove back soon."

THE END

(continued from page 24)

"Dad, would you mind if I went to the mall with Mom on Saturday?" Riley asks.

"Of course not," Dad says. "I had fun with you today. It's Mom's turn."

"Great!" Mom says. "Since it's spring, I thought we could get some new clothes."

"Best. Mom. Ever," says Disgust.

Inside Headquarters, Anger starts to sizzle. "Shopping?! I thought we were going to that rock-climbing place. Or to that shop with all the candy. Why do we have to go shopping?"

"What's wrong with shopping?" Joy asks. "Riley likes getting new clothes."

"Because Mom never makes up her mind!" Anger fumes. "She has Riley try on stuff over and over again. Don't you remember the Plaid Skirt Fiasco last fall? That took three hours. Three hours!"

Disgust nods. "And sometimes Mom loves clothes that just aren't in style. Like those red rubber boots. You know the ones." She shudders.

"Those boots kept our feet dry," says Joy. "Besides, Riley is a whole year older now. I'm sure Mom will let her pick out stuff she likes."

"If she makes us try on more rubber boots, I'm putting my foot down," says Disgust.

When Saturday comes, Mom and Riley head to the mall after breakfast.

"I thought we could start by getting you a new pair of rubber boots," Mom says. "It's going to be a muddy spring."

Riley is about to say something when Mom stops in front of a place called Adore Salon. In the window are photos of models with fancy haircuts. One has hair that's longer on the right side. Another has pink hair that's curled on top of her head like poodle fur.

"Wouldn't it be fun if you got a new haircut, Riley?" Mom asks.

Joy gets excited. "Great idea!"

Disgust frowns. "But Riley has nice long hair already. All the cool girls in school have long hair."

If Riley sticks to clothes shopping, go to page 120.

If Riley gets a haircut, go to page 49.

When the lunch bell rings, it's time for gym class. Riley has gym with Meg, but they avoid looking at each other.

"Scooter football today!" announces Coach Van Saders. "Alex, you're captain of the blue team. Maria, you're red team captain. Choose sides!"

Riley and Meg end up on Maria's team.

"Being on a team with Meg was so much more fun when we were friends," says Sadness.

"Meg is still our friend," says Joy. "Sometimes there are bumps on the friendship road. This is just a little bump!"

Tweet! Coach Van Saders blows his whistle, and Riley starts scooting across the floor. Maria throws the ball to her. Riley moves her legs as fast as she can toward the other team's goal. But a blue team player zooms toward her, ready to block her.

"Duck!" Fear yells, covering his head.

Riley sees that Meg is open. She throws her the ball. Meg catches it and zips over the blue team's goal line.

"Score!" Riley yells. She scoots over and high-fives Meg. Meg smiles. And just like that, everything is all right again.

"I told you we were still friends," says Joy.

After gym, Meg asks Riley, "Hey, we don't have hockey practice tomorrow. Want to get together?"

"Oh no," says Sadness. "Riley is supposed to see Sara tomorrow."

"Just cancel with Sara!" Disgust says. "We don't want to mess things up with Meg again."

Joy's eyes light up. "I have a good idea, guys. Trust me on this one."

If Riley cancels her plans with Sara, go to page 58.

If the Emotions trust Joy's idea, go to page 103.

"So, Ms. McGuire asked me to try out for the play," Riley tells Meg. "I don't know, I've never done that before. It might be fun."

Meg nods. "You should try it. Good luck!"

Sara has been listening. "Oh, Riley, I'm so glad you're trying out! Come on, we should get to the auditorium."

Riley texts her dad. TRYING OUT FOR THE SCHOOL PLAY. SKATE SOME OTHER TIME?

OF COURSE! Dad replies. TEXT ME AFTER AND I'LL PICK YOU UP.

Then Riley follows Sara to the auditorium. Ms. McGuire is there, along with a bunch of kids. Everyone seems excited.

Ms. McGuire quiets everyone down. "Our spring play is called *Funky Fairy Tales*," she announces. "Make sure you sign in. I'll call you up in groups to read some parts of the play."

Riley and Sara sign in and wait to be called.

"I'm so nervous," Sara whispers.

But Riley is pretty calm.

"This is so exciting!" says Joy. "We've never done anything like this before."

"This is terrifying!" says Fear. "We've never done anything like this before!"

Riley and Sara are called, along with two other kids. Ms. McGuire has them act out a scene from the fairy tale about the three little pigs.

"Riley, you're the Big Bad Wolf," Ms. McGuire says.

"Now, *that's* a part we can sink our teeth into!" says Anger.

Riley really gets into it, growling like a wolf.

"Hey, little pig, let me in your house!"

Sara makes a perfect scared little pig, shivering and shaking with every word.

"Nice job, guys!" Ms. McGuire says. "I'll post the cast list tomorrow."

"Tomorrow?" asks Disgust. "I can't wait that

long! What if we don't get the part?"

"Riley would probably cry for days," says Sadness.

That night, Mom and Dad ask Riley about the audition.

"I think I did pretty well," Riley says.

"This is exciting, Riley!" says Mom. "I used to make the costumes for all of the plays when I was in high school. If you get a part, I'll ask Ms. McGuire if I can help out."

"Ugh. Mom at school? What if she shows everyone those baby pictures of Riley she has on her phone?" Disgust wonders.

As soon as Riley gets to school the next day, she sees the cast list in the hallway.

BIG BAD WOLF: RILEY ANDERSON

FIRST LITTLE PIG: SARA PEARCE

"Woo-hoo!" Riley cheers.

After school, Riley shows Dad the script and the schedule that Ms. McGuire gave her. Dad looks at the schedule and frowns.

"What's wrong?" Riley asks.

"This is going to be tricky, Riley," he says. "You have play practice three days a week. But the travel hockey team practices on the same days. You'll have to go right from play practice to hockey practice."

Inside Headquarters, Riley's Emotions are freaking out.

"Uh-oh," says Fear. "Riley can't do both! She won't have time to eat! Or sleep!"

"No sleep? She's going to look like a zombie every day!" wails Disgust.

"It's such a shame," says Sadness.

"Of course Riley can do both," says Joy. "She can do anything!"

If Riley tries to do both, go to page 37.

If Riley sticks to hockey, go to page 64.

"Follow the sign!" Riley says.

Dad turns off the road and follows the sign to the Frog Museum. It's a tiny house painted bright green!

Inside, a woman wearing all green and sporting a frog hat greets them. "Welcome to the Frog Museum!" she says.

"Thanks," Dad says.

Riley looks around. The museum is filled with shelves loaded with all kinds of frogs: bobblehead frogs, stuffed frogs, plastic frogs, wind-up frogs.

"It's Frog-a-palooza!" she whispers to Dad. He laughs.

"Hey, Riley," he says. "How did the frog die?"

"How?" Riley asks.

"It croaked!" Dad replies. Riley cracks up.

"Hey, Dad," Riley says. "What's a frog's favorite kind of music?

"What?" Dad asks.

"Hip-hop!" says Riley. Now it's Dad's turn to laugh.

Riley and Dad make frog jokes the whole time at the Frog Museum. Before they leave, the frog lady tells them about a great diner down the road. Riley and Dad drive to the diner and order burgers that come with the best onion rings ever.

"I'm glad we followed that sign," Riley tells Dad. "This was a great day."

Sadness sighs. "And now it's all over. Bummer."

Joy grins as a gold sphere comes down the shoot. "It might be over, but Riley will always have this happy memory!"

THE END

After the half, Coach Cricket sends Riley back to the goal.

"Come on, Riley!" Anger says. "We're not afraid of any Penguins!"

"But they've already scored two goals against us," Fear reminds him.

"Not the right time, Fear," whispers Joy.

Riley stares down the ice. She keeps her eye on the puck as it zips back and forth between the Otters and the Penguins. Then one of the Penguins gets the puck and races toward her. Riley's grip tightens on her goalie stick.

Whoosh! The puck zooms toward her.

Slam! Riley stops it cold with her stick.

"Take that, Penguins!" Anger shouts.

Then Riley passes the puck to Meg. Meg swiftly makes her way toward the Penguins' goal. She passes the puck to Stacy, who's open. Stacy sends it sailing past the Penguins' goalie's ear. The Otters score!

It's a great game. In the end, the Otters beat the Penguins 4-3. Inside Headquarters, a gold, glowing sphere rolls down into the tube.

"Hooray! A happy hockey memory!" cheers Joy. "All because we tried something new."

THE END

"Meg, I'm sorry," Riley says. "You're a good friend. It's just . . . it hurts my feelings that Emily invited you and not me."

"Well, I'll ask her if you can come," says Meg.

Disgust makes a face. "Nuh-uh. No way. If Emily didn't invite Riley, we should just ignore it. Act like it doesn't bother us."

"But it DOES!" says Anger.

"Parties are notoriously dangerous, gang. I think we should just pass either way," says Fear.

"I don't know," Riley tells Meg. "Isn't that a little weird?"

But the next day, Riley and Meg are at lunch when Emily walks by. Meg calls her over.

"Can Riley come to your party?" she asks.

"This is beyond humiliating," groans Disgust.

"Well," Emily says. "This party is only for girls who are eleven."

"Are you *kidding* me with this?" Anger pounds his fist on the console.

"We're never going to be eleven!" wails Sadness.

Riley can't believe it. "But Meg is ten! Just like me."

"Well, I'm turning eleven in two weeks," Meg says quickly. "Emily says that's close enough."

"Well, I'm turning eleven in four months," says Riley.

Emily rolls her eyes a little. "All right. You can come," she says, and walks away.

"Who does this girl think she is?" asks Disgust.

Anger is not happy, either. "She doesn't even WANT us to come! Why should Riley go to Emily's party after she insulted us?"

"But we'll have fun if Meg is there," Joy says.

If Riley goes to the party, go to page 33.

If she doesn't go to the party, go to page 59.

"Um, Mom, I don't think pink is going to work for a wolf," Riley says.

Mom looks thoughtful. "I suppose you're right," she says. Then she brightens. "I know! I can dye it brown!"

Riley is relieved. She's even more relieved the next day, when she sees Meg on the school bus. Meg is in a good mood.

"I'm really sorry again about yesterday," Riley says.

"That's okay," Meg says. "I know you're really busy."

"See?" says Joy. "Isn't she a great best friend?"

Then Meg takes an envelope out of her backpack. "Mom and I planned my birthday party yesterday. It's going to be awesome. We're going to the arcade at the mall, and then to the pizza place."

"Awesome!" Riley says, and she opens the

envelope. Then she sees the date. The party is two weeks away—the same day as one of the dress rehearsals for the play. She's not supposed to miss dress rehearsals.

"Don't say anything!" Fear cries. "If we don't go to Meg's birthday party, she'll never forgive us!"

"I wish we could do both," says Joy.

"But we can't," Sadness reminds her.

If Riley goes to Meg's birthday party, go to page 47.

If she goes to the dress rehearsal, go to page 101.

(continued from page 106)

Riley walks up to the security guard.

"Excuse me," she says. "I can't find my dad."

The guard looks down at her. "No problem, little lady," he says with a kind smile. "We'll have you found in a jiffy."

He takes out a phone and to Riley's surprise, snaps a picture of her. He presses a button, and then . . . BAM! Riley's face is on every screen in the computer expo. And there's a big word underneath her: *LOST*.

Disgust groans.

Dad comes running up. "Riley! There you are," he says. "I got distracted by that battery. Sorry."

"See! We found Dad," says Fear. "Totally worth it!"

THE END

Riley and Meg go to a movie. Riley has a great time. But the next morning, she has to wake up and go right to her hockey game against the Penguins.

"Push it, girls, push it!" Coach Cricket yells as Riley and her teammates fly across the ice.

Meg makes the first goal against the other team. But in the second half, the Penguins score two goals.

Riley is starting to feel tired. As the clock winds down, one of her teammates, Haley, steals the puck. Riley skates into an opening and Haley passes to her. Riley stops the puck and shoots it right at the goal.

But the puck fizzes out as it gets close, and the goalie easily stops it.

Buzzzzzzzz! The buzzer rings, and the game is over. The Penguins win—and the Otters lose.

"How disappointing," says Sadness.

"Want to go out for pizza?" Meg asks Riley. Riley remembers her homework. "No, I have to finish my book report."

"Finish? She hasn't even started. She's gonna flunk! I don't want to live in a basement. Too many cobwebs," Fear says nervously.

"That's enough!" says Anger. "Riley is doing too much. Who goes to the theater anyway? Only people without Internet. Let's quit this dumb play!"

If Riley quits the play, go to page 124.
If Riley sticks with the play, go to page 128.

(continued from page 45)

Riley puts down the phone just before Meg comes in.

"Did you find the crayons?" Riley asks.

Meg rolls her eyes. "Under the couch."

"So, um, are you doing anything special next weekend?" Riley asks.

"Why? Are you?" asks Meg.

Riley shakes her head. "No."

"Well, me neither," says Meg.

"She's lying!" says Anger. "Emily's party is next weekend!"

"Maybe she just forgot," Joy suggests.

But the days go by, and Meg doesn't say anything. Riley sees her whispering with Emily and some other girls in the hallway at school.

The day of Emily's party comes. Riley texts Meg. **WANT TO HANG OUT TONIGHT?**

Meg texts back, **DOING SOMETHING WITH MY MOM.**

"That is a HUGE lie!" fumes Anger.

"Well, maybe there's a good reason," says Joy. "We should ask her."

The next day, Riley and Meg have a hockey game. Riley is so angry that she doesn't talk to Meg the whole game. Then, after the game is over, Riley blows up in the locker room.

"Why did you lie to me last night?" she asks.

"What do you mean?" says Meg, but she looks nervous.

"I *know* you went to Emily's party," Riley says. "You are such a liar!"

Meg's eyes fill with tears. She grabs her bag and rushes out of the locker room.

"Oh no!" says Joy. "We should go after her!"

"Yeah, we hurt her feelings," adds Sadness.

"So what? Let her go," says Anger. "*She's* the one who should apologize to *us*."

If Riley follows Meg, go to page 112.

If she doesn't follow her, go to page 53.

"Coach, I think I'm a better center," Riley tells her.

"You know, you're right," says Coach. "I need you out there scoring goals."

Madison ends up taking over as starting goalie. A player named Libby starts off as a wing. Libby and the other wing, Meg, stay on the outside of the ice while Riley skates up the center.

After a few more practices, it's time for the Otters' first game against the Penguins. Riley is excited.

"Those Penguins aren't going to know what hit them," Anger says.

"What if they're better and faster than us?" Fear worries.

"Do you think we should just hide in the locker room and cry?" asks Sadness.

"The Otters are a solid team. We're going to do great," says Joy.

Riley's heart is pounding as she faces the Penguins' center on the ice. The referee blows the whistle.

Slam! Riley gains control of the puck. She races across the ice. One of the Penguins' defensive players is guarding her pretty tightly. She sees Libby open, so she shoots the puck to her . . . and Libby lets it slide right past her! The Penguins get control of the puck.

"How did she miss that? It was perfect!" yells Anger.

The Otters get control of the puck again. Meg passes to Riley. Libby is open again, so Riley passes it—and Libby misses it again!

"Oh, come on!" Anger is fuming!

The next time Riley has the puck, she doesn't pass to Libby. Not even when she's open. During a break in the game, Coach Cricket skates up to Riley.

"Riley, you need to be passing more," she says.

"But Libby keeps missing them!" Riley protests.

"You need to give her a chance," Coach says, and Riley nods.

"Coach knows best," says Joy.

But back on the ice, Riley gets the puck and zips toward the goal. Libby is right by the net.

"Over here!" she cries.

"No way!" Anger says. "We are not passing to her again! I don't care what Coach Cricket says."

If Riley passes to Libby, go to page 29.

If Riley tries to make the goal on her own, go to page 51.

(continued from page 55)

Riley skates right past Meg, all the way to the other side of the rink.

"Hey, aren't you and Meg going to do your dance?" Dad asks. "They're playing your song."

"Meg's here with Emily," Riley mumbles. Mom and Dad look at each other and raise their eyebrows.

Fear wrings his hands. "What if Meg never speaks to Riley again?"

Sadness sighs. "Riley will probably never have another best friend again."

Dad rests a hand on Riley's shoulder.

"Don't worry," he says. "You two will make up soon enough."

"I hope it's really soon," says Fear.

THE END

Riley doesn't say anything to Meg right away. She waits until about a week before the party. Then, at lunch, she says, "Meg, I have dress rehearsal the day of your party. We're not supposed to miss it."

Meg rolls her eyes. "Seriously? So you're not coming to my party?"

"I just can't," Riley says. "I'm really sorry." Meg doesn't say another word all through lunch.

"Meg looks really upset," says Sadness.

"She'll come around," says Joy. "She's Riley's best friend."

The rest of the play rehearsals whiz by. Soon it's opening night. Riley looks in the audience for Meg but doesn't see her.

"I guess she's still mad at Riley," says Sadness.

"Then we'll make it up to her," says Joy. "Now that the play is over, Riley can spend more time with Meg. Things will be back to normal in no time."

"Do you think it will work?" Fear asks nervously.

"I know it will," Joy says.

THE END

continued from page 78

"Okay, let's do this!" says Joy.

"I'm supposed to hang out with Sara tomorrow," Riley tells Meg. "We should all hang out together!"

Meg nods. "Sara is so nice. Yeah, let's do that."

"Victory!" Joy cheers.

The next day, Riley and Meg go to Sara's house after school. Sara has a huge collection of board games. They play a crazy charades game, eat popcorn, and have a great time.

"This is awesome," says Joy. "Two best friends are better than one!"

A golden happy memory rolls into Headquarters.

THE END

(continued from page 32)

"Let's keep going, Dad," Riley urges. "I'm sure you can find it."

"I think I'd better check my phone for directions," says Dad.

He pulls over to the side of the road and fiddles with his phone. In a few minutes, they're back on the highway.

Riley sees a sign. "Dad, look! The computer expo's up ahead!"

Dad drives into the busy parking lot of the convention center. He and Riley walk up to the entrance. People push and bump into them as they get in line.

"Riley should hold Dad's hand," Fear says. "What if she gets lost?"

"Please," Disgust says, rolling her eyes. "Riley is ten and a half. She's too old to hold Dad's hand."

Finally, they get to the end of the line and enter the expo. There are big screens all over the giant room, showing the latest video games and computer programs. Dad's eyes are wide behind his glasses.

"Look, Riley! An entirely new lithium battery design!" he says.

Disgust yawns. "Fascinating."

Dad is talking to a woman in a suit about the battery. Riley looks around. Then she sees it—a hockey video game is playing on a big screen just down the aisle!

Riley tugs on Dad's sleeve. "Dad, hockey!"

"Sure, Riley," Dad says, still looking at the battery.

Riley makes her way down the aisle, weaving through the crowd. Then she finds it: the booth showing **Extreme Ice III**, the latest version of her favorite ice hockey game.

"Awesome!" says Riley. "Dad, can we try it out?"

Dad doesn't answer. He's not there!

"Dad?" Riley calls. She looks down the aisle, but it's packed and she can't see him.

Fear starts to freak out. "We're lost! I told you! We should have held Dad's hand!"

"Calm down!" Anger yells. "Dad will find us. That's his job."

"What if he doesn't, though?" Sadness asks through her tears.

On the screen, Joy sees a security guard at the end of the aisle. "We should go to the security guard. He'll find Dad for us."

"Are you serious?" Disgust asks. "That's something only a little kid would do. We should stay here. Dad will find us."

If Riley stays where she is until Dad finds her, go to page 125.

If Riley tells the security guard she's lost, go to page 92.

"So you don't think I'm a real friend?" Meg asks.

Riley starts texting her mom. "I think I should go now," she tells Meg.

"Fine," says Meg.

Riley waits on the front steps for Mom to pick her up. It's cold out. Mom is there in a few minutes.

"What happened?" she asks.

"I don't feel like talking about it," Riley answers.

The next day, Meg and Riley sit together on the bus. They don't talk to each other.

"We should say something," says Joy.

"Not until she apologizes," insists Anger.

"But what if she *never* apologizes?" asks Fear.

Riley doesn't talk to Meg all morning. Then, at lunch, she walks into the cafeteria and sees

Meg sitting at Emily's table! She can't believe it.

"We need to find a place to sit. Now! Quick!" Disgust says, in a panic. "If Riley sits by herself at lunch, her social status will never recover."

"There's Sara," says Joy. "Let's sit with her."

Sara smiles when Riley sits next to her. "Hi, Riley," she says. "Where's Meg?"

"Oh, she's at another table," Riley says, like it's no big deal. Then she changes the subject.

"So, did you try out for the play?" she asks.

"I did," says Sara. "I got a part. I'm one of the three little pigs. I'm not very good at making pig noises yet, though."

"You just need to practice," says Riley. She makes a funny, loud snorting sound. Sara cracks up.

Riley and Sara talk and laugh all during lunch.

"See? This worked out great," says Joy.

"I miss Meg," says Sadness.

The bell rings. Sara says to Riley, "Hey, do

you want to hang out after school tomorrow?
I don't have play rehearsal."

Go to page 77.

Riley tries out for goalie. She guards the goal while Coach Cricket has every member of the team try to shoot past her. There are sixteen girls on the team—and four of them score.

Madison and Ava also try out for goalie—and about half the team scores against them.

"Great job, both of you," says Coach Cricket. "Riley, you'll start, and Madison and Ava can back you up."

"Hooray!" cheers Joy.

At the next few practices, Riley gets ready for her new position. She has to learn how to keep her eye on the puck at all times. It's not easy when it's moving so fast!

On Sunday, Riley has her first game as the starting goalie. It's cold on the ice, but she's sweating behind her goalie mask.

"Why is Riley so nervous?" Joy wonders.

"It's her first game as goalie," says Fear. "What if she isn't any good?"

The game starts. Things move fast.

Whoosh! A player from the Penguins shoots a puck right past her. The Penguins score.

A few minutes later, it happens again. *Whoosh!* Coach Cricket calls out Riley and puts in Madison for the rest of the half.

"This is not going to work," says Disgust.

"If my math is correct," adds Fear, "we have a seven percent better chance of survival if we quit playing goalie right now."

"Yeah, Riley should be playing center!" shouts Anger. "She's the star of the team!"

"Not getting to play is so sad," whimpers Sadness.

"Come on, you guys, Riley can do this," Joy counters. "Let's get back out there and show them what she's got!"

If Riley quits being goalie, go to page 73.

If Riley keeps trying, go to page 85.

Riley runs after Meg.

"Hey! I'm sorry! I was just really mad that you didn't tell me about Emily's party," she says.

"Well, I didn't want to hurt your feelings," says Meg.

"But you hurt my feelings by not telling me," Riley says.

Meg gets it. "Oh."

Riley takes a deep breath. "Are we good now?"

"Yes." Meg nods. "And I'm sorry I didn't tell you. It was a dumb party anyway. It would have been much more fun with you there."

Riley smiles. "Thanks," she says. "Hey, let's see if our parents will take us out for pizza."

"Phew! Crisis averted," announces Fear.

THE END

"What do you think, Riley?" Mom asks.

"Well, it's kind of a crazy game. And I'm hungry, so maybe we should just eat," Riley says.

"Thanks," Mom tells Mindy. "Good luck finding someone else."

Mom and Riley go inside All-You-Can-Eat Wings and get a table. They each order a dozen wings. Riley gets barbecue, and Mom gets medium spicy.

"Riley is going to get barbecue sauce all over her face," Disgust warns.

"Everybody here has barbecue sauce on their face," says Joy. "She'll fit right in."

In a few minutes, their plates are clean. The waiter comes by.

"Can I get you some more wings?" he asks.

Riley and Mom look at each other.

"I don't know . . . ," Mom says.

"Come on, Mom," says Riley. "What's the point of going to All-You-Can-Eat Wings if we don't eat all the wings we can eat?"

"Good point," agrees Mom. "Two more plates, please."

When Riley and Mom get home, they're both groaning. Dad comes out of the kitchen.

"Did you two have a good time?" he asks.

"A great time!" says Riley.

"I have a surprise for you two," says Dad. "I'm cooking dinner tonight."

"Awesome. What are we having?" Riley asks.

"Wings!" says Dad.

Disgust clutches her stomach. "Nooooooo!" she wails.

But Riley and Mom burst out laughing. They're laughing so hard they can't stop.

"What's so funny?" asks Dad.

Inside Headquarters, Joy grins as another golden sphere rolls out.

THE END

SORRY, HAVE TO DO MY REPORT BEFORE THE GAME TOMORROW, Riley texts back.

PLEASE? ☹ Meg asks.

But Riley sticks to her plan. **SORRY!** ☹

"Nice choice. Because doing a report is so much more fun than going to the movies," Disgust says sarcastically.

"This stinks," says Anger.

"Meg must be so disappointed," Sadness adds.

Riley works hard on her book report all afternoon. Then she goes to bed early. On Sunday morning, she wakes up full of energy.

"All right! Game day!" Joy announces.

Riley is in a great mood when she goes into the locker room to gear up for the game. She sees Meg.

"Hey, Meg!"

Meg looks at her. "Oh, hey," she says. But she's not smiling.

"What is *her* problem?" Disgust asks.

"What's wrong?" Riley asks.

"I really wanted to go to the movies with you yesterday," Meg said. "And you didn't come to my house the other day, either. It's like you're too busy for me."

"Is she really giving us attitude right now?" Disgust asks. "Why can't she understand that Riley is busy?"

"Well, the play takes up a lot of time," Riley says.

Meg looks a little less mad. "I guess."

"Hey, I know," says Riley. "There's no hockey practice this Thursday. And I don't have play practice, either. How about I come over then?"

Meg smiles. "Cool."

Riley feels great. The Otters win the game that day!

"What a great day!" says Joy. "We won the

game, and we made up with Meg!"

But at Monday's play rehearsal, Ms. McGuire makes an announcement.

"We're having a special rehearsal on Thursday so that everyone can get fitted for their costumes," she says.

Most of the kids cheer. Costumes are exciting. But Riley groans. Meg is going to be upset all over again!

Riley quickly texts her—but Meg doesn't text her right back. Riley knows that's a bad sign.

On Thursday, Riley and the other kids in the cast go to the auditorium for the costume fittings. Mom is there with some other parents. She waves at Riley.

"We get to see our Big Bad Wolf costume!" says Joy. "This is going to be awesome."

Riley's mom waves her over.

"Riley, check this out," Mom says.

She holds up a furry pale pink costume. Riley is confused.

"What's this?" Riley asks.

"Well, we're trying to keep costs down, and I found this bunny costume in the thrift shop. I'll cut the ears short to look like a wolf."

"But it's pink," Riley says.

"And it's a fairy tale," says Mom. "A wolf can be pink in a fairy tale, right?"

Disgust isn't having it. "No. Just no. Riley needs to say something. We wouldn't be caught dead in that."

"But we'll hurt Mom's feelings," Sadness says.

If Riley says something to Mom, go to page 89.

If she doesn't say anything, go to page 25.

(continued from page 76)

"Can we just stick to shopping?" Riley asks.

Mom nods. "Sure, Riley. It's your hair."

"That's a good sign," says Joy. "I think Mom will let Riley pick out her own clothes, too."

Anger is pacing back and forth. "We are NOT trying on anything more than once."

"And no rubber boots," says Disgust. "No tight collars. No ruffles. And no more vests!"

Mom brings Riley to the shoe store first and goes right for the rubber boots. She picks up a red pair with black spots and a ladybug face.

"Aren't these adorable?" she asks.

Riley spots some cool-looking black ones. "How about these?" she asks.

Mom frowns. "But these are so cute."

"But I like these. And they'll keep my feet dry. That's the most important thing, right?"

Mom nods. "You're right, Riley. And I hate to admit it, but you're not a little girl anymore. You should be able to pick out your own clothes."

Riley smiles. "Really?"

"Really," says Mom.

The rest of the morning goes better than Riley expected. She picks out two pairs of jeans and two cute tops and Mom only makes her try each one on once! By lunchtime, they're walking through the mall with their shopping bags.

Mom points. "Look! All-You-Can-Eat wings. Are you hungry?"

Riley's stomach growls. "Very!"

They head for the restaurant, and a woman walks up to them holding a clipboard.

"Hi there," she says. "I'm Mindy, with the *Splash!* show. Do you watch it?"

"I love it!" Riley replies. *Splash!* is a local TV game show where kids and their parents compete in crazy challenges.

"Well, we're filming right here in the mall today, and we're looking for contestants," Mindy says. "Do you want to play?"

Mom and Riley look at each other.

Inside Headquarters, Disgust is shaking her head. "We all know if you lose the game you end up getting dunked in a tub of chocolate pudding. Gross!"

"But it's the best show ever!" Joy says. "We have to do it!"

"Excuse me! Did we all forget that our stomach is growling?" Anger asks.

If Riley and Mom do the game show, go to page 68.

If Riley and Mom go to All-You-Can-Eat Wings, go to page 113.

Riley breaks the news to Ms. McGuire that she's quitting the play.

"I understand, Riley," the teacher says. "But I'm disappointed, too. You made a great Big Bad Wolf."

"Thanks," Riley says.

A few weeks later, Riley sees the play during an assembly at school. Jerome Harris is playing the Big Bad Wolf.

"It's too bad Riley's not up there, having fun," says Sadness.

But the next day, the Otters win their game—and make the playoffs!

"Woo-hoo! The playoffs!" Joy cheers.

"Oh, boy," says Fear. "One day Riley's down, and the next, she's up! Is her life always going to be like this?"

THE END

Five minutes later, there's no sign of Dad.

"He's not coming," Fear insists.

"He's going to leave us behind and go home without us," adds Sadness.

Suddenly, Dad appears in front of Riley, out of breath.

"There you are," he says. "Sorry. I couldn't tear myself away from that lithium battery."

"That's okay," Riley says, relieved. "So can we try this out?"

"Of course!" Dad says.

Riley and Dad each grab a controller and start to play **Extreme Ice III**. Their game appears on the big screen overhead.

Whoosh! Riley sends a puck whizzing past Dad's goalie.

"Nice one!" Dad congratulates her.

Then Dad's player gets the puck and speeds toward Riley's goal. She tries to block him, but he zips past her.

"You're too fast!" Riley says.

A guy wearing an EXTREME ICE III T-shirt walks up to them. "You guys are good. Do you want to enter our tournament?"

Riley and Dad look at each other. "Yes!"

"A tournament! This is exciting!" Joy says.

Riley and Dad play the game against two teenage boys—and they win! Then they move on to play the next team. It's a woman and her seven-year-old grandson—and they're really good. Riley and Dad play hard but they lose the game.

"Sorry, Riley," Dad says. "I couldn't block that last goal."

Riley smiles. "I don't care. That was really fun."

Dad takes Riley's hand. "Let's go find a hot dog or something. I'm famished."

Inside Headquarters, Fear points. "See, everyone, hand-holding!"